High above the street,
where birds sang in a choir—

KAROO KAROO

a cluster of kicks swung from a wire.

Red kicks, green kicks, yellow kicks, blue.
How'd they get up there? Only birds knew.

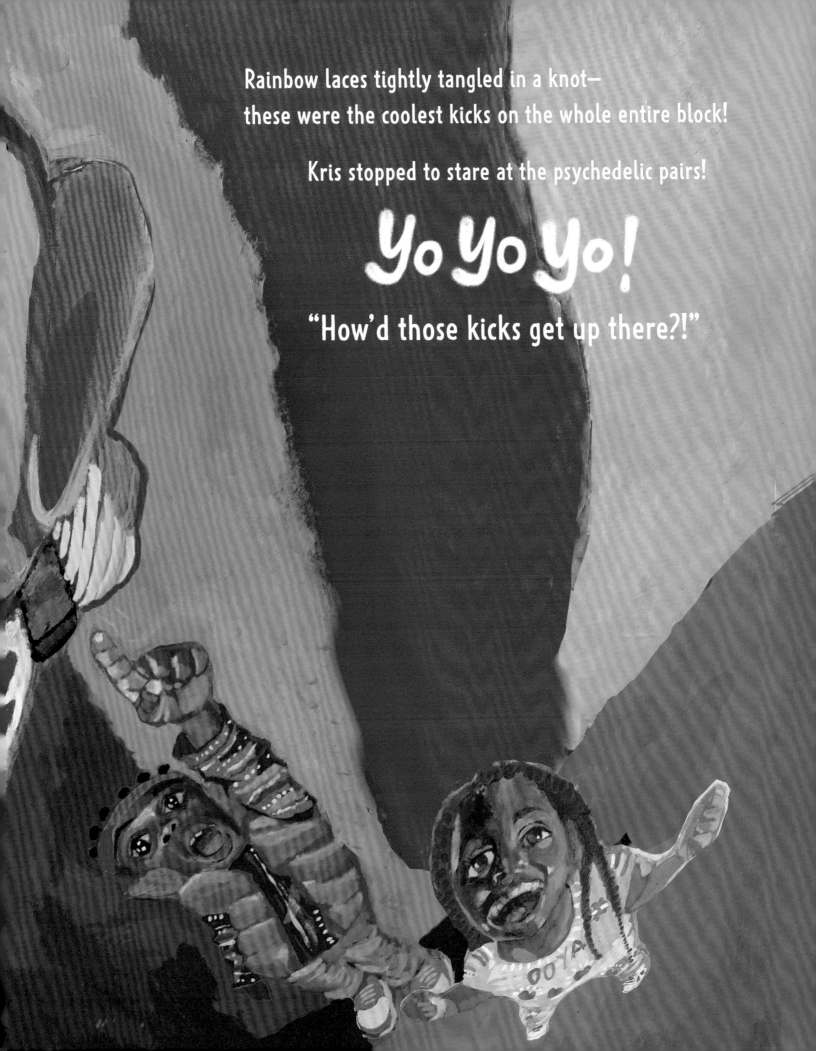

Rainbow laces tightly tangled in a knot—
these were the coolest kicks on the whole entire block!

Kris stopped to stare at the psychedelic pairs!

Yo Yo Yo!

"How'd those kicks get up there?!"

VROOM VROOM

A motorbike parade zoomed by.
The loud VROOM VROOM rattled birds into the sky!

FLAP FLIP!

Pigeons fled and the wire bounced around.
The kicks went flying and landed right on the ground.

Red kicks, green kicks, yellow kicks, blue.
The kids picked apart twisted knots on the shoes.

Twist, tug, yank. One, two, three!
Soon the rainbow laces were all tangle free!

Blue kicks, green kicks, orange kicks, red.
Would you rock yellow kicks? Or purple instead?
Danny picked a pair, fixed the laces and straps,

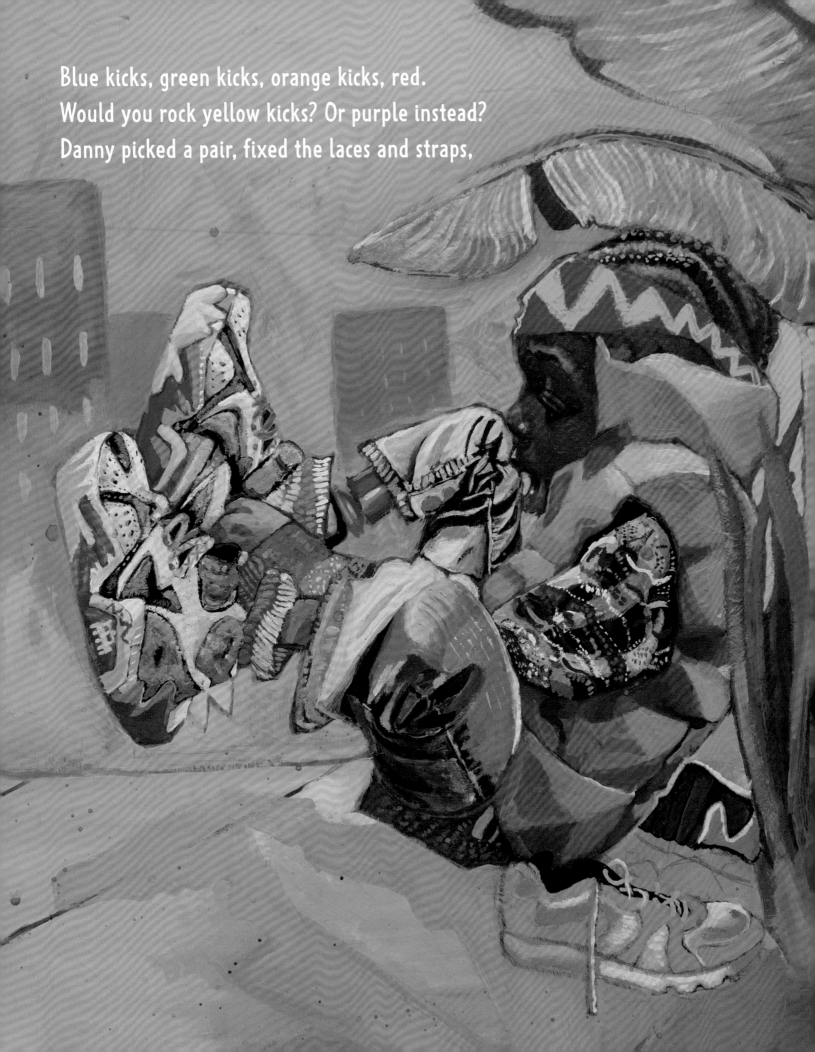

then Danny danced the shuffle
while friends hollered and clapped.

Strangely enough, Danny never learned to dance.
But his feet moved to beats, in a magical trance.

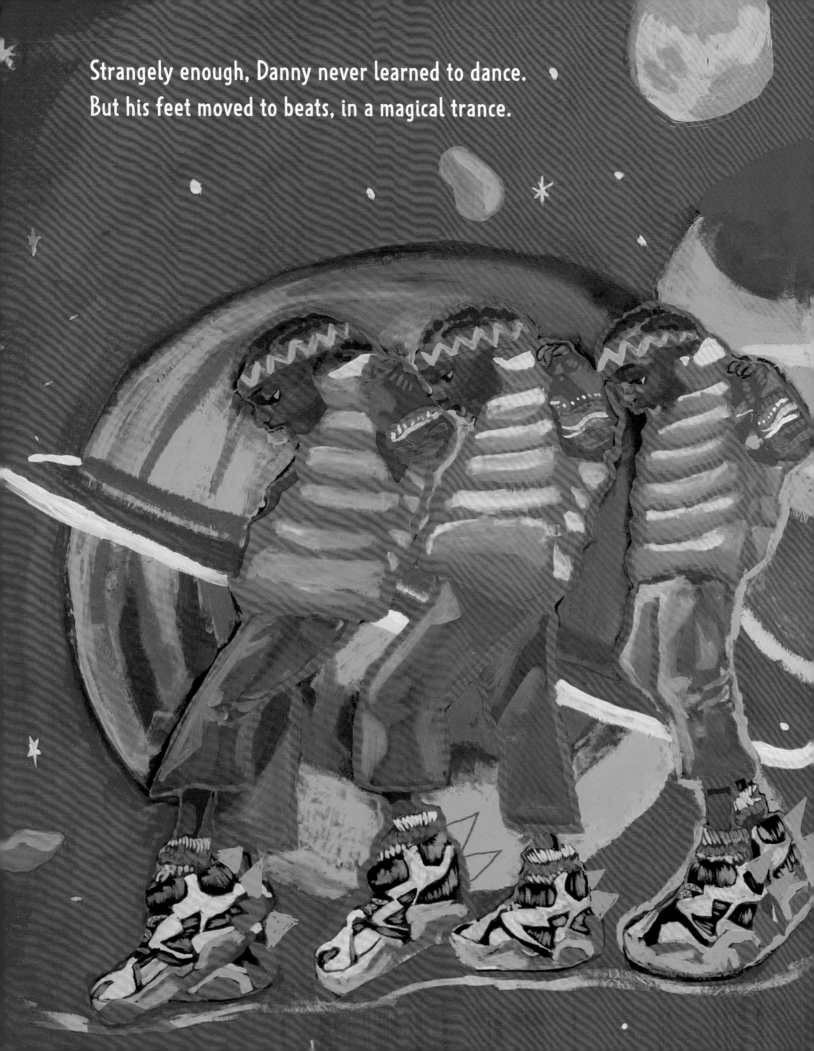

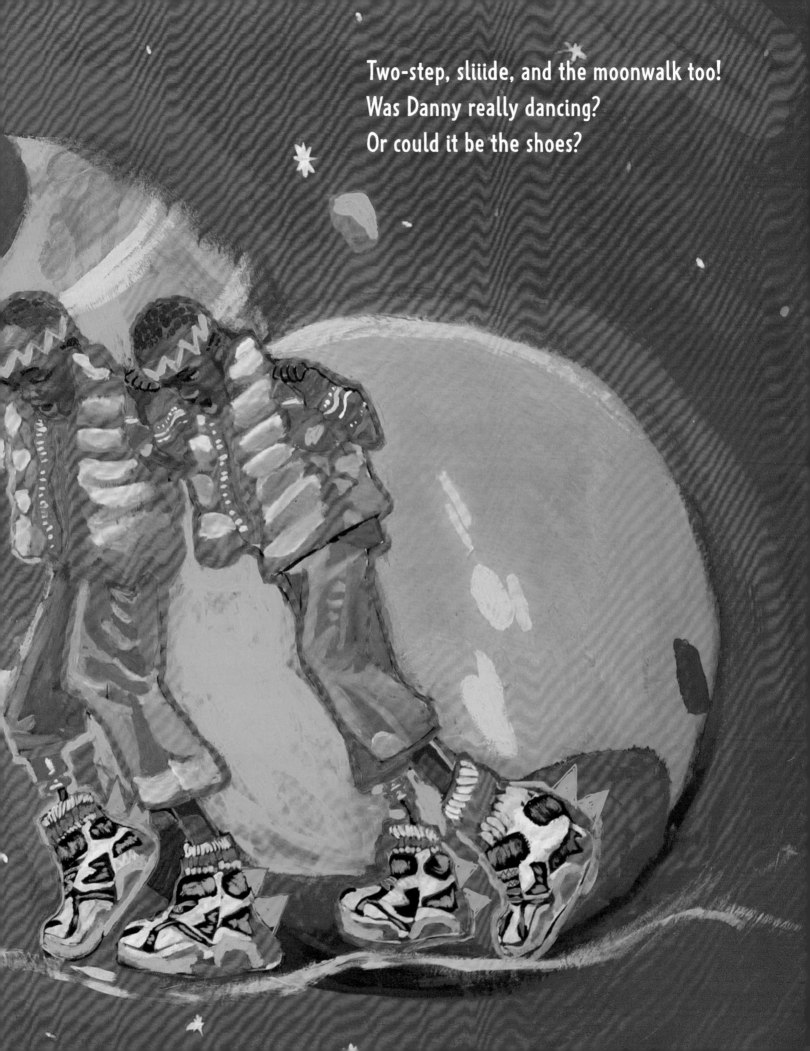

Two-step, sliiide, and the moonwalk too!
Was Danny really dancing?
Or could it be the shoes?

Kris tried a pair with a
pump on the tongue.
She pushed the pump twice,
then started to run.

Suddenly Kris jumped high into the sky.
Over a truck, along birds flying by!

SLAM DUNK SLAM DUNK

The kids began to chant.

"I CAN'T PLAY BALL!"
Kris yelled with a pant.

But her friends passed the ball as
she jumped to the rim,

Lili found a pair way too big to wear,

so instead she wore a kick like a helmet, over her hair.

She found a skateboard and now knew every trick.
Ollie, heel, flip!
Could it be her magic kicks?
Why would such amazing shoes be hung up in the street?
Who wouldn't want these cool kicks on their feet?

Botanica lady shrieked, "Those kicks are possessed!
By people who loved them but were then laid to rest."

"Aliens hung them there!" yelled Nancy from upstairs.
"I saw their spaceship drop down a couple pairs!"

El Buhonero cried, "Those kicks were hung up on the street
so that all the goons and goblins knew where to meet!"

Pigeon-coop kid squawked loudly from the roof,
"Jump and dance in the shoes if you wanna know the truth!"

He tossed a bunch of crumbs like confetti in the air.
They sprinkled every kick, peppered every pair.

KOo Koo!

More kicks fell while birds scrambled for the bread.
Now other kids could try them on their feet or on their heads.

Some people wore mismatched pairs just for fun.
Their kicks began to glow as the moon replaced the sun.

READY, SET...

Go!

The kids jumped, ran, and danced. Break-dancing in midair! You'd think they were flying at a glance.

Rainbow laces fluttered like streamers in the wind
as soles flew through clouds and to the street again.

They still weren't sure why these kicks were hung about,
so they tossed them back up for future kids to figure out.

Red kicks, green kicks, yellow kicks, blue.
How'd they get up there? Only birds knew.

To Azalea and Dior
—C.G.E.

Katherine Tegen Books is an imprint of
HarperCollins Publishers.

Kicks in the Sky
Copyright © 2023 by C. G. Esperanza
All rights reserved. Manufactured in Italy.
No part of this book may be used or reproduced in any
manner whatsoever without written permission except in
the case of brief quotations embodied in critical articles
and reviews. For information address HarperCollins
Children's Books, a division of HarperCollins
Publishers, 195 Broadway, New York, NY 10007.
www.harpercollinschildrens.com

Library of Congress Control Number: 2022930400

ISBN 978-0-06-297623-9

The artist used acrylic, gouache and oil paint
to create the illustrations for this book.
Hand lettering by Guillermo Vigil. Typography by Rachel Zegar.
23 24 25 26 27   RTLO   10 9 8 7 6 5 4 3 2 1
First Edition